UNDEAD PETS

RETURN OF THE HUNGRY HAMSTER

For Alice and Archie—SH

For Louie, the fearless
hamster wrangler—SC

GROSSET & DUNLAP
Published by the Penguin Group
Penguin Group (USA) LLC, 375 Hudson Street, New York, New York 10014, USA

USA | Canada | UK | Ireland | Australia | New Zealand | India | South Africa | China

penguin.com
A Penguin Random House Company

Text copyright © 2012 by Sam Hay. Illustrations copyright © 2012 by Simon Cooper. All rights reserved. First printed in Great Britain in 2012 by Stripes Publishing. First published in the United States in 2014 by Grosset & Dunlap, a division of Penguin Young Readers Group, 345 Hudson Street, New York, New York 10014. GROSSET & DUNLAP is a trademark of Penguin Group (USA) LLC. Printed in the USA.

Library of Congress Cataloging-in-Publication Data is available.

ISBN 978-0-448-47795-4   10 9 8 7 6

UNDEAD PETS

RETURN OF THE HUNGRY HAMSTER

by Sam Hay

illustrated by Simon Cooper

Grosset & Dunlap
An Imprint of Penguin Group (USA) LLC

CHAPTER ONE

Joe spotted the battered old jeep as soon as he turned in to his street that Saturday afternoon. Splattered with mud, its paint was peeling, its license plate was hanging off, and its roof rack groaned with trunks and boxes. Joe grinned; it could only belong to one person— Uncle Charlie! A wave of excitement swept over him, and he ran the rest of the way home.

"Joe? Is that you?" Mom called as he slammed the front door. "We've got a visitor."

Joe raced into the living room, not

bothering to take off his sneakers, which were still muddy from playing in the park. And there was Uncle Charlie, lounging on the sofa sipping a cup of extra-strong black coffee.

"Joe!" he said, beaming. "How are you, buddy?" He stood up and gave Joe a bear hug. "You've grown! You're nearly as tall as me!"

UNDEAD PETS

That wasn't strictly true—Uncle Charlie still towered over Joe. As always, Joe's great-uncle was wearing an old khaki safari suit and had his gray hair slicked back, and even though he was pretty ancient (if you counted wrinkles the same way as tree rings, he'd be about the same age as a great oak!), his eyes sparkled with energy.

"Uncle Charlie's just back from Egypt," said Mom. "Look what he brought me!" She held up a beautifully carved wooden camel.

"Cool," said Joe.

Joe thought his uncle Charlie was amazing. He was an archeologist and spent most of his time abroad, digging up old relics. Usually they wouldn't hear anything from Uncle Charlie for months, then suddenly he'd turn up on their doorstep with tales of lost cities and secret temples and treasure . . .

"So, what was Egypt like?" asked Joe.

"Hot! Very hot! And fascinating, too!"

UNDEAD PETS

Uncle Charlie replied. "We found a lost pyramid buried underground. Imagine that, Joe—a three-thousand-year-old tomb containing lavishly decorated sarcophagi, golden statues, a chariot as big as a bus . . ."

"Mummies?"

Uncle Charlie grinned. "Of course!"

"Wow!" Joe loved hearing about Uncle Charlie's adventures. He was already drifting off into a daydream about the secret pyramid and the treasures hidden within, when Uncle Charlie nudged him playfully, bringing him back to the real world with a bump.

"Now, I want to hear all about you, Joe. What's been happening? Have you gotten that dog yet?"

Joe's mom grimaced. "Don't mention the *D* word. That's all I hear from morning to night!"

"Every kid should have a dog." Uncle Charlie winked at Joe.

"Exactly!" said Joe. "That's what I keep saying!"

Mom frowned. "But I only have to hear the word *pet* and I start sneezing!" As if to prove the point, she wrinkled her nose, blinked twice, and then gave a loud *ACHOOO!*

Joe scuffed the carpet with his foot. It didn't matter how desperate he was for a dog; with Mom's allergies, he had no chance.

"Cheer up, Joe!" said Uncle Charlie. "Go and look in my bag. I've got something for you."

Joe brightened. Uncle Charlie always brought back the most amazing gifts. Once, he'd given Joe a tiger's tooth that he'd had to dig out of his own thigh. Then there was the super-spooky glass eye that had belonged to a long-dead pirate—it sat on top of Joe's dresser, eyeballing anyone who dared enter his room.

"Look for the old cigar box—it's in there."

Joe rummaged around inside Uncle Charlie's battered old leather satchel and found a few notebooks, a pair of socks, and quite a lot of sand . . . Then he spotted the cigar box. He flipped open the lid and peered inside.

"Wow, it's, um . . . great," said Joe. He lifted a shiny black stone out of the cigar box and peered at it closely. It was roughly cut in the shape of an animal.

"What is it?"

"It's an amulet, Joe. A real amulet! Ancient Egyptians used to carry them for good luck."

Joe held the amulet. It fit snugly in the palm of his hand and it felt warm and heavy. He stroked it with his thumb. The more he looked at it, the more he liked it. He especially liked the shape. "Does it have a dog's head?" he asked.

Mom rolled her eyes and laughed.

Uncle Charlie smiled. "Not a dog—a jackal! It represents Anubis, the Egyptian god of the dead."

"Cool!" breathed Joe. He couldn't wait to show it to his best friend, Matt.

Just then, Mom peered out of the living-room window. "Aha! Looks like the rest of the clan are back from the store. I'll make another pot of coffee."

As she bustled off with the coffee cups, Uncle Charlie leaned closer. "That amulet has been around a long time, Joe," he said quietly, "and it's very special. It'll grant you a wish."

A wish? Joe looked up in disbelief. He could spot a prank a mile off!

"It's true. Trust me. But only one, so careful what you wish for, because it will come true."

At that moment, the living-room door flew open, and Joe's brother and sister thundered into the room.

"Uncle Charlie!" cried Toby. "Have you brought me a dinosaur bone?"

Uncle Charlie laughed. "Not this time, Toby. But when I find one, you'll be the first to hear about it."

Joe slipped the amulet into his pocket. There was no way he was going to ask Uncle Charlie any more about it with Toby and Sarah around.

Hours later, after a noisy dinner and some amazing stories about Egypt, Uncle Charlie announced it was time he was going.

UNDEAD PETS

"Where are you off to this time?" Joe asked, though he knew his great-uncle wouldn't say—he never did.

"That would be telling!" Uncle Charlie said with a wink. "But I'm sure I'll have some new stories the next time I see you . . ."

He hugged them all good-bye, picked up his satchel, and stepped out into the inky night. Joe followed him to the end of the driveway.

Uncle Charlie took a deep breath. "Smell that air, Joe. There's magic and mischief about. I can feel it."

Joe grinned. "Uncle Charlie—aren't you going to tell me more about the amulet?"

Uncle Charlie stepped closer and whispered to Joe, "Just remember what I said—be careful what you wish for!" Then with one last wink, he climbed into the jeep.

The family waited on the doorstep for a few moments, waving as the jeep thundered off down the street, then went inside.

"Right!" said Mom. "Time for bed, everyone. You've already stayed up late because of Uncle Charlie's visit."

Joe went upstairs, feeling blue. Now that Uncle Charlie had gone, everything would just go back to normal. *If only I had a dog*, he thought, collapsing on his bed. *Then home wouldn't feel so dull after Uncle Charlie's visits.*

But this time everything was *not* the same as it always was—he had the amulet! He took it out of his pocket and looked at it closely. Was it his imagination, or was it shinier than before . . . and warmer, too? What if it really was a wishing stone? Then he sighed. *Yeah, just like the Easter Bunny is real.* He was ten years old, not five! But then again, what did he have to lose?

Joe grinned. He knew exactly what he wanted to wish for. "I wish I had a pet," he said softly. And then, louder, "I WISH I HAD A PET!"

Nothing happened. Feeling a bit silly, Joe tossed the amulet onto his bedside table and went to brush his teeth. A few minutes later he climbed into bed, flicked off his light, and closed his eyes, still thinking about dogs—big, furry, stick-chasing ones . . .

And that's when he heard it: a tiny scritchy-scratchy sort of a sound, coming from under his bed.

UNDEAD PETS

Joe lay stock-still, listening. There it was again. *Scritch. Scratch. Scuttle* . . .

What could it be? Mice? Rats? But then he heard a different noise, more like crunching.

Joe grabbed his flashlight (which he kept under his pillow, just as Uncle Charlie recommended). He leaned down and shone the light under the bed. He gasped. It wasn't a mouse, or a rat, or a spider. It was . . .

CHAPTER TWO

It was a hamster! Well, sort of. It looked like a hamster, but it was kind of green around the edges. And its eyes were odd. They were big and red and staring, like it had been watching too much TV. Joe looked closer and realized it was chewing the laces of his sneakers.

"Hey! Stop that!" he said, annoyed.

The creature froze, blinking in the light. Joe reached out to grab it, but just then it gave a loud *ACHOOO!* and sneezed all over his hand.

UNDEAD PETS

Hamster snot! YUCK! Joe wiped his hand on an old sock that was lying on the floor. Then it sneezed again—an even bigger sneeze this time— and one of its eyeballs shot out!

ACHOO!

"Rats!" squeaked the creature. "I hate it when that happens! Shine your flashlight that way a bit, so I can find it."

Joe gasped. Was he losing his mind, or had the hamster just spoken?

"Got it!" squeaked the hamster, grabbing its missing eyeball. It dusted off the eyeball and shoved it back in place. "My name's Dumpling, and I need your help!" The hamster waddled out from under the bed and bowed low. (Well, as low as his big belly would allow.) "You're Joe, the Keeper of the Amulet of Anubis, aren't you?"

"I . . . um . . . ," Joe stammered.

But the strange-looking hamster was already distracted. He sniffed the air. "Chips! I smell chips!" he said, rubbing his belly hungrily. Dumpling waddled over to Joe's book bag. He rifled through the contents, pulled out an empty bag of sour-cream-and-onion chips, and peered inside. "Crumbs!" he said, tipping the bag up and emptying it into his mouth. As the final crumb disappeared down his gullet, Dumpling let out a huge stinky *BURP*!

"Ugh!" groaned Joe. "That's disgusting!"

"Onions always do that to me," squeaked Dumpling, tossing away the empty bag and wiping his greasy paws on his tummy. "Now, where were we? Oh yes—you're Joe, the Keeper of the Amulet of Anubis, which means you've got to help me."

"What? Why?"

"Because you've got the amulet, and I'm undead!" The hamster closed its eyes and stuck out its tongue, making a "corpse" face. "I need your help before I can cross over to the afterlife. Otherwise I'll be stuck here on earth—forever!"

Joe rubbed his eyes and blinked a few times. This couldn't be happening. He couldn't really be talking to a zombie hamster . . . could he?

"You see," squeaked Dumpling, "I've got unresolved issues."

Joe frowned. "Unresolved what?"

"Unresolved issues—you know: problems, worries—and I can't rest in peace until they've been dealt with."

Joe gulped. He must be having some sort of crazy dream. Any minute now Mom would shout "Breakfast!" and it would all be over.

Dumpling waddled toward him. "The

person who possesses the Amulet of Anubis has a duty to help undead pets like me. Anubis is the protector of the dead, and you wished for a pet on his stone, so you've kind of volunteered for the job."

"Now, wait a minute," said Joe, suddenly feeling a bit annoyed. Wishing for a pet was one thing, but helping zombie hamsters with their "unresolved issues" was another matter altogether!

But the hamster didn't seem to be listening. It picked up a pen from the floor and took a bite.

HEY! STOP THAT!

"Put that down!" cried Joe.

"I always eat when I'm anxious—I can't help it." Dumpling frowned. "You see, I'm worried that Oliver, the boy who owned me, will be sad without me." He took another bite out of the pen. "And I'm not even sure his parents told him what happened to me—how I died, I mean. What if Oliver blames himself for my death?"

"Hang on," said Joe, trying to make sense of what he was hearing. "Why would he do that?"

Dumpling was about to finish off the pen when Joe made a grab for it. But as he did, the furry creature sneezed, and a hail of snot, pen bits, and chip crumbs splattered onto Joe's hand.

"Ugh! Gross!"

Dumpling shrugged. "I can't help it! It's the dust that makes me sneeze—my fur's full of it." To prove his point, the hamster jumped up and down, and a huge cloud of dust formed around him.

This time Joe sneezed. "Stop it! Stop it!"

"Don't you want to know why I'm so dusty? It's a very sad story."

"No, I don't want to know why you're so dusty," said Joe irritably, rubbing his nose.

But as he spoke, Dumpling the hamster sneezed again, blasting Joe with another shower of snot.

Joe gritted his teeth. "Look," he said as politely as he could, "I think maybe you should leave. You know—go off to hamster heaven, or wherever it is dead pets hang out."

"I've already told you," squeaked Dumpling angrily. "I can't! I'm an undead pet, and I'm not going to be dead until you've helped me!"

"I can't help you," said Joe.

"But you must! You're the Keeper of the Amulet of Anubis! You've got to help me make sure Oliver is okay—and that's that!"

UNDEAD PETS

The hamster folded its little front legs and scowled at Joe.

Joe had had enough. "Well, we'll see about that!" He picked up the amulet, which was still lying on his bedside table, and marched over to the window. He slid it open, muttered, "Sorry, Uncle Charlie," and threw the amulet out into the night.

"There!" he said. "I'm no longer the Keeper of the Amulet, so you can go and bother someone else!" And with that he climbed back into bed and turned off his light.

"If you'd just listen to my story...," whined the hamster.

"No!" Joe pulled the covers up over his head.

"But you must!"

"No!" Joe yelled again. "And stop talking! Go to sleep or something."

"Sleep?" Dumpling squeaked. "Don't you know anything about hamsters? We're nocturnal. I'll be wide awake all night."

Joe sighed and buried his head under his pillow.

"Stop messing around!" squeaked the hamster. "I need your help, and I need it now!"

Joe groaned.

"GET OUT OF BED AND HELP ME!"

Joe peeked out from under the pillow to find Dumpling standing at the end of his bed looking very annoyed.

Joe reached out, grabbed a dirty sock

from the floor near the bed, and threw it at the hamster. "Put a sock in it!" he snapped.

THWACK! The hamster toppled off the end of the bed with an angry squeak.

For a moment or two there was blissful silence, but then Joe heard a familiar munching sound. Dumpling was doing exactly as he'd been told. He was putting a sock in it—in his mouth, to be precise! "Mmmm," he mumbled. "Tasty!"

Joe sighed and pulled the pillow back over his head.

CHAPTER THREE

When Joe opened his eyes early on Sunday morning, he briefly wondered whether it had been a bad dream. But then he noticed little dusty footprints all over the room, and tiny bite marks on everything—the bottom of the curtains, his book bag, even his underpants!

Dumpling, however, was nowhere to be seen.

Cautiously, Joe climbed out of bed, opened his bedroom door, and peered out at the landing. There was no sign of the little pest, but Joe did spot something else. The Amulet of Anubis was sitting on top of the bookcase.

Just then, Joe heard a gnawing sound coming from the bathroom. He pushed open the door and found Dumpling sitting in the empty bath, eating Joe's mom's pink sponge.

"Hey, stop that!" Joe snatched it out of the hamster's mouth.

"Don't shout at me," Dumpling spluttered. "If you'd have helped me when I asked you to, instead of just ignoring me, then I wouldn't still be here!"

The hamster hauled himself up the side of the bathtub using the plug chain as a rope. Then he started sniffing around Mom's bubble bath. "Mmmm, strawberries . . ."

"Leave that alone!" exclaimed Joe.

"Everything okay, Joe?" Dad's head peeked around the door. "Thought I heard you talking to someone."

UNDEAD PETS

Joe gulped. He wasn't sure how he was going to explain the hamster to Dad. He turned around, blocking Dumpling from his father's view.

"Hey, did you see your amulet?" asked Dad. "It's on top of the bookcase. I found it outside this morning when I went to collect the paper. You must have dropped it when you were saying good-bye to Uncle Charlie."

sniff sniff!

So that was how it had reappeared!

"Yeah, thanks, Dad."

Just then Dad noticed the mangled sponge in Joe's hand. "What on earth have you done to that?"

From behind Joe, Dumpling burped loudly. Joe flinched.

"Well, you see," Joe stuttered, "I, um . . . well, I sort of used the sponge to clean my cleats last night."

Dad sighed. "I've told you to clean your cleats outside, Joe, and you know you shouldn't use a bath sponge. There's a scrubbing brush in the garage for that sort of thing. Your mom's going to be mad!"

"Sorry. I'll buy her another one."

"Good idea. And don't do it again!" Just as Dad turned to go, the hamster jumped off the side of the bathtub, darted between Joe's legs, and skidded across the bathroom floor toward Joe's father.

UNDEAD PETS

"Stop!" Joe yelped.

Dad turned around. "What?"

"Um . . . well . . . ," said Joe, staring in horror at Dumpling, who was now sniffing around Dad's slippers as though he was about to have a nibble. "Don't!" Joe yelped.

Dumpling rolled his eyes. "Okay, okay."

Dad frowned. "Don't what? What are you talking about, Joe? And why do you keep looking at my feet?" Dad glanced down to see if he'd stepped in something.

Dumpling, meanwhile, waddled back into the bathroom and shimmied up the towel rack. "He can't see me or hear me, Joe," he squeaked. "Only you can. Look, I'll show you!"

The hamster stuck out his tongue and blew an enormous wet raspberry at Dad.

Joe gasped. But Dad didn't even blink.

"I haven't got all day, Joe. When you've remembered what it was you wanted to say, come and find me." Shaking his head,

Dad left the bathroom.

Joe breathed a sigh of relief. "That wasn't funny!" he hissed. "And now I'm in trouble over the sponge."

Dumpling shrugged. "It's not my fault. I told you, I always eat when I'm worried."

"Well, stop worrying!"

"I CAN'T! Not until I know Oliver is okay. The sooner you start helping me, the sooner I'll stop eating and be out of your way. After all, it's your duty as the Keeper of the Amulet of Anubis!"

"Will you stop going on about that stupid amulet?" Joe scooped up the hamster and went back to his bedroom. He put Dumpling down on his desk, then got dressed as fast as he could.

"Stay out of trouble!" he said to the hamster as he tied his sneakers and headed for the door. "I'm going to get rid of the amulet once and for all!"

UNDEAD PETS

When Joe returned to his room a while later, Dumpling was waiting for him with a smug smile. "There's no way around it, Joe—this is your duty! Are you going to help me now?"

Joe sighed. He didn't seem to have much choice! He had tried everything. First, he dropped the amulet down a drain outside his house, but some workmen were cleaning the drains, and one of them saw Joe's "accident" and fished the amulet out for him. Next, Joe buried it in the backyard, but his neighbor's cat dug it up and left it on Joe's doorstep.

Then he tried flushing it down the toilet, but his little brother spotted it in the bowl and pulled it out for him!

But Joe wasn't beaten yet. He raced back downstairs, sneaked into the living room, and turned on the computer. He wasn't supposed to use it without telling his parents, but this was an emergency! He opened his mom's e-mail account and found Uncle Charlie's address. His great-uncle didn't check his e-mail much—he didn't usually have Internet access on his travels—but it was worth a shot. Joe began to type . . .

Dear Uncle Charlie,

    I made a wish on the amulet, but it's gone a bit wrong! How do I undo the wish? Please e-mail or call soon.

Thanks!

Love, Joe   **SEND**

Just as Joe hit SEND, he heard a small voice saying, "Joe . . . Joe . . . ," and Dumpling climbed up onto the desk next to him.

Joe shook his head. There had to be a way to get out of this wish. Suddenly, another idea came to him: the Internet! Of course! You could find out anything on the Internet—there must be some information about the amulet somewhere.

"How do you spell *Anubis*?" asked Joe, opening the web browser.

Dumpling shrugged. So Joe just typed it how it sounded. Hundreds of search results popped up, lots of them about Anubis, the Egyptian god of the dead. But one in particular stood out:

The Legend of the Amulet of Anubis.

Joe clicked on the link. As the page loaded, he felt a surge of excitement; surely now he'd find a solution to his hamster problem. At the top of the page was a rough sketch of his amulet: black, shiny, and jackal-shaped. And next to it there was a description . . .

The Legend
of the
Amulet of Anubis

The Amulet of Anubis is a stone carved in the likeness of Anubis, the jackal–headed Egyptian god of the dead. (Anubis is also known as the Conductor of the Souls or Keeper of the Dead.) Anubis was said to have invented the process of mummification, and he was worshipped as the protector of the dead. Legend says the amulet is endowed with special powers, granting the bearer a single wish—a wish that cannot be undone!

"Rats," muttered Joe.

"Told you so!" said Dumpling smugly. "So, are you ready to help me now?"

But Joe didn't get a chance to argue, because just then there was a shout of "Breakfast!" from the kitchen.

Joe scooped up the hamster and opened the desk drawer. Pushing aside pens, tape, and a hole puncher, he shoved Dumpling inside. "Now, stay there and be quiet!" he said as he shut the drawer firmly. "And try not to eat anything. I'll be back soon."

CHAPTER FOUR

"There you are, Joe," said Mom. "It's not like you to be the last one to the table. Certainly not when your dad's frying up a breakfast feast!"

"Yeah, I was just . . . in the bathroom."

"What do you want for breakfast, Joe?" called Dad, as he put some bacon in the frying pan. "Toast? Or the works: bacon, eggs, and hash browns?"

Joe's mouth watered as he breathed in the smell of the frying bacon. "Toast and the works, please!"

He was just about to sit down when a little voice squeaked, "WATCH OUT!"

It was Dumpling.

Joe's heart sank. "I told you to stay put!" he whispered as Dumpling climbed up onto the table.

Sarah peered over the top of her magazine and raised an eyebrow at her brother. "Who are you talking to, twerp?"

"Oh, um . . . no one."

"What's for breakfast?" asked Dumpling.

Joe sat down, glaring at the hamster. "Get off the table!"

Sarah put down her magazine. "Seriously, who are you talking to? Your imaginary friend?" She giggled.

"I don't have an imaginary friend!" Joe snapped.

"I told you, they can't see or hear me," said Dumpling. "Look."

UNDEAD PETS

To Joe's horror, Dumpling waddled across the table toward Sarah and jumped up and down, raising a dust cloud around him. Sarah carried on reading, totally oblivious to the zombie hamster leaping around the table.

"Here you go, Joe," said Mom, handing him a plate of toast spread with her homemade jam. Joe's stomach growled—his favorite! But as he reached for the toast, Dumpling made a dive for it, too, and it quickly began to disappear.

UNDEAD PETS

"Slow down, Joe!" Dad laughed as he returned to the table with a plate of bacon and eggs for Sarah. "You've eaten half your toast in ten seconds flat!"

"Maybe his imaginary friend is helping him," Sarah said with a smirk.

"Come on, Sarah," said Dad. "Leave your brother alone."

Joe scowled at his sister. She was almost as much of a pain as Dumpling, who was now licking jam off his sticky paws.

chomp chomp!

UNDEAD PETS

The hamster turned to Joe. "So, shall we get started on finding Oliver?"

"I'm not going to help you!" Joe hissed.

"He's doing it again," said Sarah. "Did you hear him, Dad? He's talking to himself like a five-year-old!"

Toby, who was six and had been happily talking to himself for the last ten minutes, made a face at her. So did Joe. But before a fight could break out, Mom came over to the table. Then her nose twitched, her eyes watered—and she sneezed loudly! "Has the neighbor's cat been in here?" she said, rubbing her eyes.

Dad shook his head.

"Perhaps Joe's imaginary friend is making you sneeze, Mom," said Sarah. "Maybe he's a big hairy collie dog."

If only! thought Joe. But then it occurred to him—maybe Sarah wasn't too far from the truth. Could it be Dumpling setting off Mom's allergies? She couldn't see him, but could she somehow sense him?

Mom's eyes were streaming now, and her nose had turned red. Joe had to get Dumpling as far away from her as possible. He picked up the hamster and stuffed him into his pocket (much to Dumpling's annoyance).

"Here we are!" said Dad, handing Joe a full plate. "The works!"

"Sorry, Dad, I can't eat any more. I feel a bit sick after eating the toast so quickly. You have it," he said. Joe leaped to his feet and dashed to his bedroom before Dad could stop him.

"I had to miss breakfast because of you!" he hissed, dropping Dumpling onto his desk.

Dumpling huffed. "If you'd just listen, I would explain why I need your help."

"Right!" snapped Joe. "I'm listening now."

Dumpling was quiet for a moment, and then he began . . .

"I was six weeks old when I went to Oliver's house.

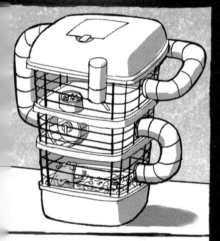

He gave me an amazing home . . .

and loads of treats!

So many treats that I got too fat for my tunnels.

One day, his mom cleaned out my cage and accidentally left the door open. I couldn't resist the chance to explore.

I didn't spot the vacuum cleaner until it was too late."

ACHOO!

"It's all very sad," said Joe. "But I still don't see how I can help you."

Dumpling plucked a pencil out of Joe's desk drawer and nibbled it. "It's Oliver I want you to help. I don't think he knows it was his mom who left my cage open." Dumpling gnawed harder. "He must be wondering how it happened. And he'll be so, so lonely without me—it's already been a week since the accident."

Joe frowned. "So you want me to make sure Oliver is okay? That's it?"

The hamster nodded.

"Do you know where he lives?"

"No, but the badge on his book bag looks just like the one on yours."

"You think he goes to my school?" Joe racked his brain for any Olivers he could think of. "I think Toby has a friend called Oliver . . ."

Dumpling suddenly brightened. "That might be him! I know, tomorrow I'll come to school with you and point him out."

"Maybe . . . ," said Joe, who wasn't sure he wanted to take Dumpling to school.

But Dumpling was happy (for the moment, anyway). He yawned, emptied out the rest of the pencils from the drawer, and climbed inside it. "Tomorrow we'll go to school," he said sleepily. "And we'll see Oliver and make sure he's all right . . ." His eyes began to close. And then, as though someone had pressed a SLEEP button, Dumpling was suddenly snoring.

Joe sighed. *Hamsters! Up all night, asleep all day!* Dogs were definitely much better pets. He tiptoed out of his room and back downstairs to see if there was any bacon left.

CHAPTER FIVE

Thankfully, Joe saw very little of Dumpling for the rest of the day. Dad took him and Toby swimming while Mom and Sarah went shopping, and later they all met up for dinner at his grandparents' house.

It was past seven o'clock when they got home. Dumpling was waiting for Joe in his room. The hamster was wide awake and excited.

"I can't wait to see Oliver tomorrow!" he said, dancing across the desk toward

Joe. "Once I've made sure he's all right, I'll be able to cross over to the afterlife." He twirled and whirled . . . until he reached the edge of the desk and fell off into Joe's trash can.

"Okay, okay, I'll take you to school," said Joe, trying not to laugh as he fished Dumpling out of the trash. "Just try to keep the noise down tonight. I need to get some sleep before school. And don't eat any of my stuff!"

Dumpling crossed his heart. "Thank you! Thank you! I'll be good, I promise."

And he was, sort of. While Joe slept, Dumpling amused himself in one of Joe's drawers by building himself a den. (He only nibbled a couple of socks.) Then he explored the closet and found lots of boxes and board games. (He only swallowed two dice and three chess pieces.) And then there was Joe's gym bag to rummage in, where the hamster found an old apple core and a banana peel that kept him going until dawn.

By the time Joe woke up the next morning, Dumpling had dozed off in his sock-drawer den. Joe had just enough time to get dressed, eat his breakfast, and check his mom's e-mail for a reply from Uncle Charlie (there wasn't one) before the peace was disturbed. Joe was in the hall putting on his shoes for school when there was a big banana-scented *BURP!* in his ear.

"Is it time to find Oliver?" said Dumpling, climbing into Joe's book bag.

Joe nodded. Then he whispered, "Just stay in there and keep quiet. And don't eat my lunch, okay?"

Once Toby was ready, he and Joe set off for school. They hadn't even gotten to the end of the street before Dumpling started moaning.

UNDEAD PETS

"Can't you walk any faster?" he squeaked, poking his head out of the bag. "Hurry up! We need to find Oliver! QUICK!"

Joe gritted his teeth. "Shut up!"

"Who are you talking to, Joe?" asked Toby.

But Joe didn't have to reply because his best friend, Matt, appeared. He waited for them at the corner of their street every morning.

"Hey." Matt grinned. "Good weekend?"

Joe made a face. "I've had better!"

Joe ignored Dumpling for the rest of the journey, and talked to Matt about video games.

UNDEAD PETS

As they turned in to the schoolyard, Dumpling suddenly let out a loud squeak. "There he is! There's Oliver! The boy in the green coat, playing basketball!" And then, after a pause, he added in a small, disappointed voice, "The boy who is laughing and joking . . . and doesn't look sad at all."

Joe scanned the playground and spotted Oliver. "Hey, Toby, is that your friend Oliver?"

"Where? Over there? Yeah, that's him."

"Do you know him well?" Joe asked, trying to sound casual.

"I'm going to his house after school tomorrow." said Toby. "Why?"

UNDEAD PETS

But just then the school bell rang, and Joe dashed off to his classroom.

"Don't worry," he whispered to Dumpling as he stuffed his bag under his desk. "I'll go and find Oliver at recess."

But Dumpling couldn't wait that long. He needed to know why Oliver wasn't sad! As soon as class had begun and Joe was distracted, the undead hamster climbed out of the bag and waddled off.

It was almost ten o'clock by the time Joe realized Dumpling was missing.

"Oh no!" he muttered, looking around the room. Joe could imagine what mischief Dumpling would be getting up to. He sighed. Somehow he'd have to get out of class and try to find him.

"Excuse me, Miss Bruce," he said, raising his hand. "Can I go to the bathroom?"

His teacher peered over the top of her spectacles. "Can't you wait until recess?"

Joe crossed his legs and made a face. "No! I'm desperate! I think I might wet my pants."

This made everyone laugh. Well, everyone except Miss Bruce, but she let him go anyway.

Luckily, Dumpling had left a tiny trail of dusty footprints. Joe followed them down the corridor, past two classrooms and the boys' bathroom, until they disappeared into the kitchen. Joe swallowed hard. Kids weren't allowed in there, but he had to find Dumpling! He slipped inside, darting behind a tower of trays as two lunch ladies appeared.

"I don't understand it," one was saying. "I left two dozen peanut-butter-and-jelly sandwiches on the counter, and now six of them have disappeared!"

UNDEAD PETS

Joe rolled his eyes. *DUMPLING!* But there was still no sign of the little hamster. Then Joe spotted more footprints—only these had peanut-buttery edges! They led out the other side of the kitchen, through another door. Crouching down so the lunch ladies wouldn't see him, Joe sneaked through the kitchen and followed the trail out of the door, past the girls' bathroom and the janitor's closet, to where it ended, right outside the principal's office. Surely Dumpling hadn't gone in there?

Joe took a deep breath and knocked. He wasn't sure what he was going to say—*Excuse me, sir, please may I have my zombie hamster back?*—but luckily, there was no answer. Joe pushed open the door and looked around. The office was empty. "Dumpling? Are you in here?" he whispered.

And then Joe spotted him,

UNDEAD PETS

fast asleep on the desk—inside the principal's lunch box! Scattered around him were the remains of a lunch: an apple core, some sandwich crumbs, and a strawberry-yogurt container, licked clean. Dumpling had eaten everything!

"Dumpling!" Joe yelled. "What have you done?" He raced across the room and grabbed the sleepy hamster. "Wake up!"

"Joe Edmunds! What are you doing in here?"

Joe gasped. Mr. Hill, the principal, stood in the doorway, scowling.

CHAPTER SIX

Joe gulped. "Um . . . well, you see, sir, I spotted a mouse in the hallway, and it ran under your door. I knocked, but you weren't in, so I decided to come in and try to catch it . . . But I think it must have eaten your lunch."

Mr. Hill did not say a word.

Joe could tell that the principal was not in the mood for listening to tall tales. "Honestly, sir, it's true," he said weakly.

Mr. Hill crossed his arms, unimpressed. "I was only gone for five minutes, and even if there was a small rodent in my office, which I very much doubt, it couldn't eat an entire lunch in that time!"

You don't know what an undead hamster's capable of! Joe thought gloomily.

Mr. Hill gave Joe a stern look. "Joe Edmunds, taking—or eating—other people's property is wrong. You can stay inside during recess and think about your behavior!"

Joe shuffled back to the classroom with his head down. "I can't believe you got me into trouble again!" he muttered to Dumpling, who was stuffed inside his shirt pocket.

"I was only looking for Oliver," whined the hamster. "When I couldn't find him I got worried, and you know how hungry I get when I worry."

Joe rolled his eyes and wished for the hundredth time he'd never set eyes on Uncle Charlie's amulet.

By lunchtime, the whole school knew about the lunch-box incident. And, to make things worse, Miss Bruce gave Joe extra homework as punishment! Dumpling had nodded off in Joe's bag, but the lunch bell woke him up, and he started wriggling around impatiently.

"There's Oliver!" squeaked Dumpling as soon as they went into the cafeteria.

Joe took a deep breath. Talking to Oliver without his friends thinking he'd gone crazy was not going to be easy. Older children never ate lunch with the younger kids. Joe saw Matt and his other friends wave to him from their usual table. He waved back but kept on walking. He went over to where Toby and Oliver were sitting with a couple of other boys and pulled up a chair. "Hi," he said, feeling very silly.

Toby smiled in surprise.

The other two boys at the table nudged each other. "Is it true you stole Mr. Hill's lunch?" said one.

"Um . . . sort of," said Joe, his face turning red.

"Cool!" said Oliver, grinning.

Toby beamed, too.

"Talk to Oliver! Talk to Oliver!" squeaked Dumpling, who was bouncing up and down on top of Joe's lunch box. "Ask him about me!"

"Yeah, well, I needed a snack to keep me going," Joe said, pretending to yawn, "because I'm so tired. I was up all night working on my

school project about . . . um . . . hamsters."

Toby looked puzzled. That was the first he'd heard about Joe having a school project.

But Oliver's face lit up. "Really?"

"Yeah," said Joe. "I've got to do a survey. You know, speak to people who've had pet hamsters and ask them all about what food is best, which toys their pets like . . ."

"My hamster, Dumpling, likes his wheel," said Oliver cheerfully.

Joe frowned. Didn't Oliver mean that Dumpling *used to* like his wheel?

"But his favorite toy is definitely his hamster ball," Oliver added. "I bought it for him last weekend. He loves rolling around my bedroom floor in it!"

"What?" squeaked Dumpling. "He never bought me a ball!"

"Oh, cool," said Joe. "So you've got a pet hamster? Could I ask you some questions about . . . Dumpling?"

Oliver smiled. "Sure! What do you want to know?"

Joe pulled a pencil and a crumpled piece of paper from his bag to take notes. "Well, what about Dumpling's eating habits? Sometimes hamsters can be a bit greedy."

"Dumpling definitely is!" said Oliver. "Well, he used to be," he added, looking a bit worried. "About a week ago he suddenly got skinny, and now he can fit inside his tunnels again."

"What's he talking about?" shouted Dumpling. "I'm not skinny, look at me!"

Joe was puzzled. "Really? That sounds a bit odd."

"Yeah," said Oliver. "I thought so, too. But Mom says that hamsters often lose weight in the spring."

"But what about the vacuum cleaner?" Dumpling yelled in frustration.

Joe scratched his nose. Something weird

was going on. It sounded like Oliver thought Dumpling was still alive. But how could that be? The hamster Oliver was describing didn't sound like Dumpling. Unless it was *another* hamster . . .

That must be it! After the accident, Dumpling had been swapped for a new hamster, without Oliver knowing!

"I've been replaced!" bawled Dumpling. "And Oliver doesn't even know it!"

Joe and the hamster were in the boys' bathroom, having a quick talk before the end of recess. Since Dumpling had heard the news that he'd been swapped, he had become frantic with worry and started scarfing down everything in sight!

"Stop that!" said Joe, taking a wad of toilet paper out of Dumpling's mouth. "Look on the bright side—at least Oliver's not lonely."

UNDEAD PETS

"You've got to tell him his hamster's a fake!" Dumpling wailed.

"How?"

"I don't know. But you've got to do something. You heard Oliver—he's worried that I'm losing weight. Except it's not me, it's a skinny imposter!" And with that, Dumpling snatched up a bar of soap and started chomping. Enormous pink bubbles began to pop out of his nose.

Joe grimaced. He was no hamster expert,

but he didn't think eating soap was good for hamsters—even undead ones!

Then suddenly a nugget of an idea formed in his head. A hamster expert? That was what Oliver needed. Someone who could explain why "Dumpling" had turned skinny! Someone who could go to his house and give him some advice.

"I think I've got a plan," said Joe slowly.

Dumpling stopped chewing.

"I'm going to become a hamster expert. I'm going to learn everything there is to know about them. Then I'll offer to go around and visit Dumpling to see why he's losing weight."

"But Dumpling's not losing weight, you big dummy!" squealed Dumpling. "*I'm* Dumpling!"

"Yes, we know that—but Oliver doesn't!" said Joe, feeling exasperated. "Don't you see? Once I'm at Oliver's house I'll be able to find a way to reveal to him that his hamster's not you! But first I have to get him to invite me over, which is why I need to pretend to be a hamster expert."

Dumpling sighed. "That might work. I guess."

"It *will* work!" said Joe firmly. It had to work! If it didn't, he'd be stuck with the whiniest soap-guzzling hamster in the world, forever! And then suddenly Joe remembered something. "Of course! Toby said he was going home with Oliver after school tomorrow—that makes things much easier! I'll be able to tag along with him."

Dumpling sniffed miserably. "Hope so."

Me too! thought Joe wearily.

Luckily for Joe, he had study time in the library last thing on Mondays. He made straight for the reference section, gathered all the hamster books he could find, and then settled down to read.

UNDEAD PETS

"Did you know there are over forty different colors of hamsters?" he whispered to Dumpling, who was "working" his way through a book of his own—a very boring one about birds, which actually tasted better than it looked.

"And did you know that baby hamsters are called pups?" Joe added as Matt came over to join him.

Matt made a face when he saw Joe's book. "What're you reading about hamsters for?"

Joe shrugged. "Just curious. Hey, did you know most pet hamsters only live until they are about two years old? That's not very long, is it?"

munch!

Dumpling huffed loudly and rolled his eyes. Suddenly, Joe realized that the life span of a hamster probably wasn't the best thing to mention in Dumpling's presence. "But they have an incredible sense of smell!" he added quickly.

By the time the bell rang at the end of the day, Joe was well on the way to becoming a full-on hamster bore!

"Hey, guess what," said Joe as he walked out of school with Matt and Toby. "The smallest hamsters in the world come from Mongolia and they only grow to about two inches long!"

Matt gave him a funny look. "Uh-huh."

"And did you know that one human year is like twenty-five hamster years?"

"Yeah, yeah, whatever," said Matt.

"And did you know that hamsters originally come from the Syrian desert, where they build complex systems of deep tunnels?"

Matt puffed out his cheeks. "What is it with you and hamsters today?"

"It's because of his school project!" said Toby.

Matt frowned. "Huh? What school project?"

Joe quickly changed the topic to video games.

Meanwhile, Dumpling, who was a bit cranky from lack of sleep, spent the entire journey whining about how Oliver's mom had replaced him. "It's an outrage!" he squeaked. "Oliver's probably stuffing the new hamster with treats, trying to make it bigger. We've got to tell him what really happened!"

Joe sighed. It was going to be a long night if Dumpling kept acting like this. He was planning to check his mom's e-mail account again when he got home, to see if Uncle Charlie had replied.

But as soon as he stepped through the front door, he realized his plan would have to wait . . .

CHAPTER SEVEN

The house was in chaos! The windows were wide open, the hall rug was rolled up, and Mom was on her hands and knees scrubbing the floor.

"What's going on?" asked Joe.

"Oh, hi, boys," said Mom, looking up. Her eyes were red, and it sounded like she had a stuffy nose. "Have a good day?" She got up and gave them each a big wet kiss. "Sorry, I think we've got dust mites. Or it might be mice. I'm not sure, but I can't stop sneezing, so there must be something nasty around."

Joe groaned. *That's probably Dumpling!*

"Would you like to help me?" Mom asked. "I'll give you both some extra allowance money. Toby, you can dust the dining room."

"Yes, please!" He grinned, taking a duster from her.

"And, Joe, would you mind finishing the floor while I start on the living room?" She handed him the scrubbing brush she was holding, then went to fetch the vacuum cleaner. A moment later it roared to life in the next room.

At the sound of the vacuum cleaner turning on, there was a sudden jerk from inside Joe's book bag. Dumpling popped out of the top like a champagne cork, landing with a *thud* on the ground, and took off.

"Dumpling, come back!" hissed Joe, chasing after him into the kitchen. But he was nowhere to be seen. Joe checked the bread box, the cookie jar, and the cupboards. Nothing. Then he heard a noise coming from the freezer—a crunching, gnawing sort of a noise. Joe opened the door, and there was Dumpling, squished up in the corner, munching his way through a box of fish sticks.

"Dumpling!" said Joe. "What are you doing in there?"

"It's the only place I can't hear that terrible vacuum cleaner," wailed the hamster.

"You can't stay in there, you'll freeze!" Then Joe remembered—Dumpling was not a normal hamster, he was an undead one! "Oh right."

UNDEAD PETS

The hamster scowled at him. "Shut the door and leave me alone!"

"Well, at least stop eating all the fish sticks."

"Oh, not again!" said a sarcastic voice. It was Sarah. She shook her head. "Don't tell me—your imaginary friend lives in the freezer?"

Joe closed the door with a *thump*. "I haven't got an imaginary friend!" he snapped, and stomped back to the hall to scrub the floor.

The moment he'd finished, he sneaked back to the kitchen to check on Dumpling, but he was gone. (Along with two boxes of fish sticks, a bag of frozen peas, and half a tub of chocolate ice cream.)

"How about fried chicken for dinner?" said Mom, appearing behind him. "It was going to be fish sticks, but it looks like we've run out. Dad's going to pick up some chicken on his way home. Help yourself to a snack, in the meantime."

UNDEAD PETS

"Mom, can I use the computer?" asked Joe. "I've got to do some research for a school project about pets."

"Oh, you'll enjoy that!" Mom picked up the furniture polish. "Okay, but don't make a mess. You know how Dad hates crumbs in the keyboard."

Joe grabbed a bag of chips and a carton of chocolate milk and headed for the dining room. He knew he should be looking for Dumpling, but he was really enjoying a break from the troublesome rodent. He needed to find out more about hamsters. And most important of all, he wanted to check whether Uncle Charlie had e-mailed back!

He clicked on his mom's e-mail account. There were no new messages.

Joe sighed. Uncle Charlie was probably up to his neck in dinosaur bones or something.

He opened the web browser instead and typed *hamsters* into the search bar. He found lots of good sites, including one about health problems. It had loads of facts about hamster teeth, and that gave Joe an idea.

But he didn't have long to think about it, because the front door opened just then, and the delicious smell of fried chicken and french fries wafted through the house.

"Dinner!" Dad called.

Joe kept an eye out for Dumpling as the family sat down for dinner. He didn't have to wait long. He'd only managed one bite before the hamster hauled himself up onto the table and started chowing down.

"Mmmm, tasty!" he said, eating a whole french fry in one go, like a sword-swallower in a circus.

Meanwhile, Mom's nose had started twitching again, and Joe knew it wouldn't be long before the sneezing started. He wolfed down his dinner as fast as he could.

"Slow down, Joe," said Dad. "It's not a race."

"Yeah, Joe, you're eating like a pig!" Sarah sneered.

But Joe didn't care. He was watching Mom. Her eyes were watering now. Any minute the sneezing would start . . .

ACHOOO! Mom buried her nose in a tissue.

Joe swallowed the last of his french fries, grabbed the hamster, and stood up. "I'm just going to finish my homework," he said. And before anyone could tell him it was his turn to clear the table, he ran for it!

"You've gotten me into trouble so many

times today," Joe said when they were back in his bedroom. "I couldn't even eat my dinner."

"I can't help it. Don't you understand that I'm upset? I've been replaced!" Dumpling sulked.

"I wish I could replace you," muttered Joe. "Now stay out of trouble, or I'll grab the vacuum cleaner and finish you off myself!"

Dumpling gasped and ran under Joe's bed, looking horrified. He didn't reappear for the rest of the evening.

At bedtime, Joe dug out a bag of mini candy bars he'd been saving since Christmas. "I've put some candy out," he called. "Eat as many as you like . . ." *Hopefully they'll keep him busy for the night.*

There was no reply from Dumpling.

"Suit yourself!" Joe said as he got into bed. Moments later, he was asleep.

UNDEAD PETS

Joe awoke suddenly. *What's that noise?* He glanced at his clock. It was past midnight. He listened. There it was again—a thumping sound, coming from the kitchen. "Dumpling!" he growled.

He grabbed his flashlight and tiptoed downstairs. The noise grew louder the closer he got to the kitchen. Joe pushed open the door and gasped . . .

There was stuff everywhere! Slices of bread were scattered all over the table, an open can of baked beans was spilled across the kitchen counter, and a jar of pickled onions was smashed on the floor.

Dumpling, who was sitting in the middle of it all, looked ready to cry. "I was hungry!"

"Trying to make a mess is more like it!" Joe grabbed some paper towels and started mopping up the juice from the baked beans.

Dumpling gave a stinky burp, then put his head in his paws and blubbered. "I can't help it. I'm so worried about Oliver!"

Joe was about to reply when he heard footsteps. *Uh-oh*. It seemed like he wasn't the only one who'd been awoken by the noise!

"Joe! What's going on down here?" It was Mom. She was dressed in her nightgown, and her nose was still red from sneezing.

"Um . . . well . . . ," stammered Joe. "I was a bit hungry, so I thought I'd make a snack."

"Some snack!" Mom looked at him angrily. She was usually pretty cool about messes, but even her patience was pushed to the limit by *this* disaster! Then she sighed. "Watch out for that broken glass, Joe. I'll fetch the vacuum cleaner."

"NOOO!" Dumpling wailed. "Not the vacuum!" He took off like an Olympic sprinter and sped out of the kitchen.

Joe sighed and helped his mom clean up the rest of the mess. While she put the vacuum cleaner away, Joe sneaked a loaf of bread and some jam up to his bedroom, just in case Dumpling got the munchies before morning. But when he got upstairs, he couldn't see the hamster anywhere. He dumped the food on his desk, climbed back into bed, and fell asleep.

CHAPTER EIGHT

By the time Joe woke up, the food was gone, and Dumpling was asleep in the sock drawer, his nose stained pink from the jam.

Joe tiptoed around his room, getting ready for school. He was hoping he might actually be able to sneak off without Dumpling today, but as he picked up his bag to leave, the hamster opened one beady red eye and squeaked, "Is it time to go?"

Joe frowned. "I'm only taking you if you promise to be good."

Dumpling nodded. "I promise! Are you sure your plan will work?"

"Of course!" said Joe confidently. But he wasn't sure at all. He still hadn't worked out what he was actually going to say when he got to Oliver's house.

After a boring math class—which Dumpling spent swinging off the edge of Joe's desk by two paws, chewing a pen cap—they went outside at recess to track down Oliver.

They found him on the far side of the playground; he was kicking a ball with Toby and two other friends.

"Hey, Oliver!" Joe called.

Oliver waved. "Hi, Joe!"

"Listen, I've been thinking about what you said yesterday about Dumpling's weight loss," said Joe.

Oliver nodded, and his smile faded.

UNDEAD PETS

"Well, I've been reading hamster books for my school project, and I found a chapter on health problems," Joe continued.

"What do you think is wrong with him?" asked Oliver.

"I'm not sure. It could be a toothache. If you give your hamster too many treats, their teeth rot, and they can't eat."

Oliver gasped. "Will he die?"

"I'm dead already!" growled Dumpling.

UNDEAD PETS

Joe ignored Dumpling. "It might not be a toothache," he said, seeing how worried Oliver looked. "So, I was thinking, Toby's going to your house today, isn't he? Well, maybe I could tag along and take a look . . ."

"That would be great. I'll ask my mom after school." Oliver grinned.

Dumpling's face lit up with excitement. "I'm going home! I'm going home!" he squealed with delight.

Joe didn't dare remind him that it wasn't his home anymore and that it belonged to another hamster now!

At the end of school, Joe spotted Toby and Oliver at the gates. Oliver was talking to his mom. She looked concerned.

"Hey, Joe!" Oliver waved him over. "I was just telling Mom that you know loads about hamsters, and that you've offered to look at

UNDEAD PETS

Dumpling's teeth. Mom, would it be okay if Joe came home with us, too?"

"PLEASE! PLEASE!" Dumpling squeaked from inside Joe's book bag.

"I'm really not sure . . . ," Oliver's mom said. It looked like a visit from a hamster expert was the last thing she wanted!

"Please!" Oliver begged. "You know how worried I've been about Dumpling lately."

UNDEAD PETS

She sighed. "Oh, all right. But Joe will have to give his mom a call and check if it's okay." She handed him her cell phone.

Yes! thought Joe. He'd done it! He'd gotten an invite to Oliver's house. All he needed to do now was work out how to prove Oliver's hamster was a replacement. That was going to be a bit trickier . . .

CHAPTER NINE

After calling his mom, Joe headed to Oliver's house with Toby.

"I can't wait to show you Dumpling!" Oliver grinned.

Dumpling, who was poking his nose out of Joe's bag, groaned. "I wish he'd stop calling that imposter 'Dumpling'! I'm Dumpling!"

Joe ignored him. "So, Oliver, when did you first notice that your hamster had lost weight?"

Oliver's mom glanced at Joe.

"About a week ago, I think," said Oliver. "I

was lying in bed watching Dumpling playing in his cage, when all of a sudden he ran through one of his tunnels. He hasn't been able to do that for months!"

The real Dumpling blew a raspberry. "That's because it wasn't me!"

"Mmm," said Joe thoughtfully. "So the weight loss was very sudden?"

Oliver's mom's eyes narrowed.

"Yeah," said Oliver. "Really sudden."

"Did you notice anything else unusual about Dumpling?" asked Joe. "Like a slight change of color, maybe?"

Just then Oliver's mom coughed loudly. "So, Joe, do you have any hobbies?" she asked.

Joe tried not to smile. *You mean, apart from being an annoying hamster expert?* he thought.

After that, every time the conversation returned to hamsters, Oliver's mom changed the subject. By the time they got home, she looked flustered and fed up.

"This is my house!" said Oliver as they arrived at a bungalow with a blue front door. They went inside, and Oliver kicked off his shoes. "My room's down here. Come and see Dumpling."

"Wouldn't Joe and Toby like a snack first?" asked his mom.

At the mention of food, Joe's tummy rumbled.

Oliver frowned. "Could we have it in my room? I really want them to see Dumpling!"

Oliver's mom hesitated. "All right, then," she said wearily. "Leave your shoes and bags in the hall, boys," she said. "And look out for the vacuum cleaner—I didn't have time to put it away before I picked you up from school."

"No! Not the vacuum cleaner!" squeaked Dumpling.

Joe scooped Dumpling out of his bag and

stuffed him into his pocket, then followed Toby and Oliver to the bedroom.

Sitting on a low table under the window in Oliver's room was the hamster cage.

Wow! thought Joe. It was three stories tall, all of the levels connected by colorful plastic tubes. And on the ground floor, fast asleep in a nest of wood shavings, was Dumpling. The new Dumpling!

Dumpling wriggled around in Joe's pocket. "I can't see! Put me down!"

He took the hamster out of his pocket and set him on the table without the others noticing.

"He looks nothing like me!" said the real Dumpling. "Totally different!"

It was true—they did look different. But that was mostly because the real Dumpling was now a zombie hamster, complete with a green tinge and big, staring red eyes!

Oliver crouched down and looked at his new hamster. "He's great, isn't he?"

Toby grinned. "Yeah, he's really cool!"

"When are you going to tell him?" asked Dumpling.

Joe shrugged. He wasn't sure where to start.

Oliver, meanwhile, was tapping gently on the cage. "I'll wake him up, and then maybe you can have a look at his teeth."

Dumpling sulked off. He'd spotted something familiar on top of Oliver's dresser:

his old treat box! He started to scale the dresser like a rock climber.

Oliver reached into the cage and took out the sleepy hamster. "Want to hold him?"

As Joe stroked the hamster's fur, he decided that still-alive hamsters were definitely better than moaning undead ones! The little creature opened its eyes and snuffled Joe's hand.

"He's probably looking for treats." Oliver grinned.

"Huh!" growled the real Dumpling, who was now halfway up the dresser.

"How do his teeth look?" asked Oliver.

Joe wasn't sure how to check. None of the books had told him how to make a hamster open its mouth. "I'll just give him a minute to get used to me," said Joe, "then I'll try to take a look . . ."

Oliver nodded. "Okay, but do you think he looks healthy? I keep trying to make him eat more, to build him up again, but he's just not as hungry as he used to be."

"His eyes are bright and his coat is shiny," said Joe, repositioning his hands as the new Dumpling ran from palm to palm. "And he's certainly full of energy!"

It was true. He was a handsome hamster, exactly the right sort of weight—unlike other hamsters Joe could mention. Just then Joe heard a munching sound. He looked over to see the real Dumpling sitting on the top of the dresser, stuffing his face with little green treats. And then something else caught Joe's eye—a framed photo perched on the dresser.

Still holding the new hamster in his hands, Joe walked over to take a look. "Is that you and Dumpling?"

Oliver nodded. "That was us last Christmas . . ."

Joe peered at the picture, then looked at the new hamster. He could see that, even without the red eyes and green tinge, the Dumpling in the picture looked very different from the new hamster. "Wow, Dumpling does look different now, doesn't he?" Joe held the new hamster next to the photo. "Look at the color of his fur—it's lighter, isn't it? Even his nose is different."

Oliver's eyes widened. "That's weird."

Just then Oliver's mom came into the room, carrying a tray laden with cookies and

potato chips. "Everything okay in here?" she asked nervously.

As Joe turned to look at her, the new Dumpling wriggled through his fingers—and jumped! Joe tried to grab the hamster but missed and bumped into the dresser. As the dresser wobbled, the real Dumpling lurched sideways, knocking over the picture, which crashed onto the floor, shattering the glass inside the frame.

For just one second everyone froze. Then there was pandemonium!

"Watch out for the glass, boys!" said Oliver's mom, putting the tray down on Oliver's bed. "You've got nothing on your feet!"

But Oliver wasn't listening. "Where's Dumpling? I can't see him!"

"Which one?" said Joe, without thinking.

"Catch him!" cried Oliver as the new Dumpling scuttled around their feet.

UNDEAD PETS

"Mind the glass!" Oliver's mom yelled.

Then Joe had an idea. He raced out of the room and down the hall. He picked up the vacuum cleaner and dragged it back to the bedroom, where Oliver and Toby were chasing the hamster, and Oliver's mom stood by with a look of terror on her face.

"Keep still, Oliver!" shouted his mom again. "You're standing right in the broken glass!"

UNDEAD PETS

"Don't worry, I'll get it," said Joe. He plugged in the vacuum cleaner and switched it on.

And that's when it happened. Oliver's mom glanced from the vacuum cleaner to the hamster scuttling wildly at their feet. She waved her hands at Joe. "No! Not the vacuum cleaner! You don't want to suck up Dumpling!" she screamed. "Not like last time!"

Stop! Stop!

UNDEAD PETS

Oliver stopped in his tracks. "What?"

Oliver's mom clapped her hand over her mouth, as though she wished she could suck up the words she'd just said.

CHAPTER TEN

Joe turned off the vacuum cleaner—much to the relief of the real Dumpling, who was still on top of the dresser, frozen with fear! As soon as the noise stopped, the new hamster scuttled out from under Oliver's bed, and Joe pounced on it. "Gotcha!"

"What do you mean, 'Not like last time,' Mom?" Oliver asked.

Oliver's mom gave a huge sigh and suddenly looked almost relieved. "Oliver, I think I've got some explaining to do."

"So you see, by the time I realized what was happening, it was too late . . ." Oliver's mom sniffed. "I'm so sorry, Oliver."

Joe and Toby were sitting with Oliver and his mom in the kitchen, sipping hot chocolate. Dumpling was there, too, taking sneaky sips from Joe's mug.

Oliver frowned. "So my hamster doesn't have bad teeth?"

Oliver's mom shook her head.

"And he's not sick?"

"No."

"He's actually a totally different hamster?"

His mom looked at her hands. "I'm so sorry, Oliver. It was just a terrible accident. I must have left Dumpling's cage open after I cleaned it out. And then when I was vacuuming, he suddenly appeared and got sucked up."

UNDEAD PETS

Oliver looked horrified.

Dumpling nudged Joe. "Tell him it didn't hurt!"

"I don't think he would've suffered," said Joe. "I'm sure the end was very fast."

Oliver sighed and nodded.

His mom bit her lip. She looked close to tears, and Joe felt a bit sorry for her. After all, it was an accident, and she'd only gotten the replacement hamster because she hadn't wanted Oliver to be sad.

Then Oliver took a deep breath. "Don't worry, Mom. I do feel sad about the old Dumpling, but I know he had a good life."

"I DID! I DID!" squeaked Dumpling.

"Maybe I could clean out the cage myself from now on?" said Oliver.

Mom pulled a tissue from her pocket and blew her nose. "That sounds like a good idea."

"And maybe you shouldn't give the new pet hamster quite so many treats," said Joe, glancing at Dumpling, who was perched on the handle of Joe's mug, his head dipped down inside it to drink. "That way he'll always be able to enjoy his tunnels."

"Hey, are you calling me fat?" said Dumpling, his nose covered in hot chocolate.

Oliver's mom put her arms around her son and hugged him.

Joe scuffed the floor with his foot. He always felt a bit silly watching people hug. "I'm just going to go to the bathroom," he said.

Dumpling jumped down from the table and scampered out into the hall. Joe noticed that the hamster was looking different somehow. Not quite so green around the edges . . .

"Are you feeling okay, Dumpling?"

The hamster grinned. "It's time I was going, Joe. Now that the truth is out, I feel ready to cross over."

Dumpling seemed to shimmer slightly, growing more transparent.

"Do you need anything for the journey?" Joe asked. "Candy? Chips, maybe?"

Dumpling prodded his swollen cheek pouches. "I grabbed some of the treats from Oliver's room. I'm saving them for later. Good-bye, Joe. Thanks for everything."

Joe took the hamster's tiny paw in his hand

and shook it gently. "Good-bye, Dumpling. Um . . . good luck."

Dumpling faded, until there was only the hint of a hamster outline . . . then that disappeared, too. Joe heard a tiny burp, and all that was left of Dumpling was the faint smell of onions.

BURP!

UNDEAD PETS

A little while later, Joe's mom arrived to collect them. And after a bit more hamster talk with Oliver and a promise to visit again soon, Joe and Toby followed her out to the car.

Joe was quiet on the way home. He was relieved that Dumpling had gone, but a bit sad, too. It was the closest he'd ever come to having a pet of his own—even if he was an annoying, overeating, undead pet. When he got home, Joe went straight to the computer to send another e-mail to Uncle Charlie.

Dear Uncle Charlie,
    Don't worry, everything's fine! Can't wait to tell you about my adventure!

Love, Joe

SEND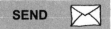

Then he headed upstairs to his bedroom. As Joe kicked off his shoes and lay down on his bed, he smiled to himself. It had been a strange few days. He'd actually had a real adventure—one that Uncle Charlie would be proud of!

It did feel good for everything to be back to normal, though. *I might even get some sleep tonight*, thought Joe, stretching out his legs and closing his eyes for a second.

And that's when he heard it. A very faint *meowing* sound, ghostly and strange. Joe sat up and listened. There it was again . . . It seemed to be coming from the garden. As though a cat were stalking around outside. But it didn't quite sound like any other cat that he'd ever heard. He was about to take a look out of his window when he heard Dad calling from downstairs: "Dinner!"

Joe grinned. *Just the wind*, he told himself firmly.

UNDEAD PETS

As Joe closed his bedroom door, the Amulet of Anubis twinkled on his bedside table. Outside, a black shadow lurked—a cat-shaped shadow. And two alarmingly yellow eyes blinked in the night, watching and waiting . . .

Joe was just an ordinary boy—
until he made a wish on a
spooky Egyptian amulet.
Now he's the Protector of
UNDEAD PETS ... and there's
a crazy cat on his tail!

Poor Pickle met her end under the wheels of a car.
Can Joe help Pickle protect her sister before
there's another catastrophe?

COMING IN NOVEMBER 2014!

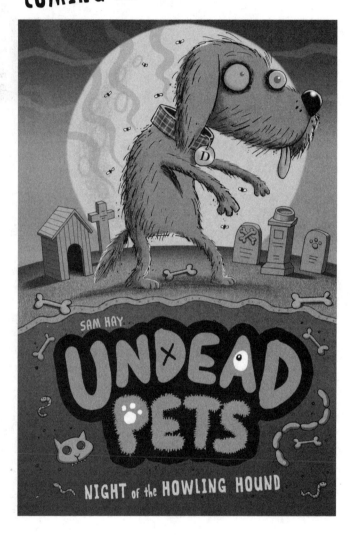